"Did you just stop by to check on us, Jorgen?" Wanda wanted to know.

Jorgen cleared his throat. "Actually, I am not on duty at the moment."

Timmy, Cosmo, and Wanda all gasped! They couldn't remember Jorgen Von Strangle *ever* being off duty!

Jorgen nodded. "I have been ordered to take some time off. It seems my superiors have noticed that I have a little vacation time saved up."

Now it was Wanda's turn to raise an eyebrow. "How much time *do* you have saved up?"

Jorgen blushed, embarrassed. "A little more than three hundred years."

Cosmo flew over to Jorgen and conjured up a banner with his wand that read BON VOYAGE. "Then you're *definitely* due for a break from looking over our shoulders! Have a great time! Don't forget to write!" Cosmo said.

Based on the TV series *The Fairly OddParents*™
created by Butch Hartman as seen on Nickelodeon®

ISBN 0-439-76093-3

12 11 10 9 8 7 6 5 4 3 2 1   5 6 7 8 9 10/0

Printed in the U.S.A.   08

First Scholastic printing, September 2005

Vacation FRUSTRATION!

BY ADAM BEECHEN

ILLUSTRATED BY BARRY GOLDBERG

SCHOLASTIC INC.

New York   Toronto   London   Auckland   Sydney

Mexico City   New Delhi   Hong Kong   Buenos Aires

CHAPTER ONE

"I wish you would steal Francis's towel," Timmy Turner whispered.

He was hiding behind a row of lockers in the gym locker room at school. Physical education class had just ended, and today's lesson had been on swimming. Francis, the class bully, snapped his towel at Timmy's friend Chester's feet. Chester hopped and danced like a jumping bean while Francis laughed.

"You know we can't do that, Timmy," Wanda, his fairy godmother, reminded him. She was in the shape of a combination lock hanging off a locker. "Da Rules say we can't steal!"

8

"Not even in this case?" Timmy griped. "Francis doesn't deserve to be protected by Da Rules! He's a bully! And he's a bully who keeps giving me wedgies in the cafeteria during lunch!"

"He sounds pretty nice to me," said Wanda's husband, Cosmo. He was Timmy's fairy godfather, and he hung from another locker—but in the shape of a bean-and-cheese burrito. "Maybe he thinks you're hungry, and he wants to share some of his yummy wedgies with you!"

Wanda gave him a look. "Wedgies aren't food, Cosmo," she whispered in his ear.

Cosmo's eyes went wide as Wanda told him what a wedgie really was. "Ouch!" Cosmo yelped. "That's definitely not yummy!"

"Anyway, we can't steal Francis's towel," Wanda told Timmy. "But you can run out there and get it yourself."

Timmy frowned and tugged

on his pink baseball cap. "And then I'd wind up dancing the cha-cha like Chester! No thanks!"

"I like the cha-cha," Cosmo cried happily, changing his shape from a burrito to a small train that puttered up the side of the locker.

"No, dear, that's choo-choo," Wanda said gently.

"What's the big deal about stealing one little towel?" Timmy wanted to know. "If it'll keep Chester from getting snapped at, then that's a good thing, right?"

Wanda shook her head. "Stealing is stealing, Timmy. And we have to follow Da Rules. Our boss, Jorgen Von Strangle, *definitely* wouldn't like us breaking Da Rules!"

Timmy peeked over the lockers. Chester's face was turning red and he was out of breath. He looked like he was about to explode! "Jorgen Von Strangle would only get mad *if* he found out!" said Timmy. "And I'm not going to tell him!"

"I think we should do it, Wanda," Cosmo urged his wife as they transformed back into their normal bodies. "We *could* use some new towels. And Jorgen probably won't find out."

Wanda nodded grudgingly. "That's true," she said. "Okay, we'll do it. I hope we won't regret this. . . ." Wanda raised her wand. Sparkles filled the air as Timmy stepped back and smiled, ready for the fun to start.

Suddenly a voice with a heavy accent spoke from behind them. "What is going on here?"

Timmy spun around, and Cosmo hid his wand behind his back. Jorgen Von Strangle stood glaring at them from an open doorway into Fairy World!

CHAPTER 2

"We weren't doing anything, Jorgen," Wanda said.

Jorgen raised one eyebrow suspiciously. "Really? Because I had a feeling you were about to break Da Rules by stealing!"

"Break Da Rules?" Cosmo repeated. "We'd never do something like that! We didn't think that what we were going to do would actually be considered stealing, so really that's just bending Da Rules a little—*ow!*" Wanda elbowed her husband in the ribs before he could finish.

Timmy pointed to the lockers. "Cosmo and Wanda were helping me with a science project, Mr. Von Strangle, sir. I was wishing for some lockers to study, and *poof*, they whipped one up for me!"

Jorgen stepped forward, the door to Fairy World

vanishing behind him. As he bent down to look at the rusty lockers, Timmy noticed for the first time that Jorgen wasn't looking very Jorgen-like today. Instead of his usual military-style clothes, he was wearing a Hawaiian shirt and shorts. And he was holding a suitcase. "These are very nice lockers," Jorgen said. "It looks like they have been here for many years." He saluted Cosmo and Wanda. "Good work!"

Cosmo saluted in response. "Back at ya, Jorgie!"

"We'll continue this little game tomorrow," Timmy heard Francis yell at Chester as they went separate ways out of the locker room. Chester was huffing and puffing. Jorgen had never seen them, and they hadn't seen Jorgen. Timmy exhaled in relief.

"Did you just stop by to check on us, Jorgen?" Wanda wanted to know.

Jorgen cleared his throat. "Actually, I am not on duty at the moment."

Timmy, Cosmo, and Wanda all gasped! They couldn't remember Jorgen Von Strangle *ever* being off duty!

Jorgen nodded. "I have been ordered to take some time off. It seems my superiors have noticed that I have a little vacation time saved up."

Now it was Wanda's turn to raise an eyebrow. "How much time *do* you have saved up?"

Jorgen blushed, embarrassed. "A little more than three hundred years."

Cosmo flew over to Jorgen and conjured up a banner with his wand that read BON VOYAGE. "Then you're *definitely* due for a break from looking over our shoulders! Have a great time! Don't forget to write!" Cosmo said.

"Where are you going to go?" asked Wanda.

Jorgen set his suitcase down and looked around. Timmy thought he looked kind of sad. "I do not know," Jorgen admitted. "My girlfriend, the Tooth Fairy, can't take a vacation right now because it's her busy season. I thought I might go visit some friends, but then I remembered . . . I do not have any other friends."

"That's terrible," Timmy said, standing in front of Jorgen. Cosmo and Wanda flew behind their supervisor so he couldn't see them, and they waved their arms and shook their heads furiously at Timmy, trying to get him to stop talking. But Timmy didn't notice. "I know you'd have a great time hanging out with us, Jorgen. I wish you could spend your vacation with Cosmo, Wanda, and me!"

Cosmo and Wanda hung their heads, but Jorgen's face lit up with a huge smile. "You have wished it, and so it is true," he said happily. "I will spend three hundred years with you! Hey, that rhymed!" He squeezed them together in a powerful hug.

Too late, Timmy realized what he had done! "Uh oh," he squeaked.

CHAPTER 3

That afternoon back in Timmy's room Jorgen quickly made a chest of drawers appear and started unpacking his suitcase. Timmy watched him take out spare wands and identical sets of military clothing.

As Jorgen worked, Cosmo and Wanda flew over to Timmy. They didn't look very happy. "Timmy, what were you thinking?" Wanda wanted to know.

"Yeah," Cosmo said, rolling his eyes. "Spending three hundred years with Jorgen Von Strangle isn't *my* idea of a vacation!"

"I'm sorry," Timmy moaned. "He just looked so sad, it seemed like the nice thing to do! I said it, but I didn't think about what I was *really* saying!"

Wanda hovered glumly next to him. "I suppose

it *was* a nice thing to do, Timmy," she said. "We shouldn't be upset with you for trying to do something nice."

"I have unpacked," Jorgen said, turning back to them and making the chest of drawers magically disappear. "What are we going to do first, new best friends?"

Timmy, Cosmo, and Wanda looked at each other, then back at Jorgen. "Well, it's your vacation," Timmy reminded Jorgen. "What do you like to do?"

Jorgen thought about it for a long time, then he shrugged. "I like to work," he said.

"But the whole point of a vacation is that you don't *have* to work," Cosmo said.

"Oh, right," Jorgen said, nodding. He scratched his head and thought some more. "I like to make sure people don't break Da Rules," he said.

Wanda threw up her arms in exasperation. "That's your job," she shouted. "What else do you like to do?"

Jorgen thought some more. Then he thought about it even more. He kept on thinking. "We could spend the next three hundred years watching Jorgen try to think of something!" Cosmo whispered to Wanda, showing her an hourglass he held in his palm.

Suddenly Jorgen clapped his hands, an excited look on his face. "I know!"

Cosmo, Timmy, and Wanda leaned in to listen. "I like to work," Jorgen told them.

Timmy and his fairy godparents huddled together. "Clearly, Jorgen doesn't know how to take a vacation," Wanda pointed out.

"It's up to us to find something he likes to do," Timmy said.

Cosmo nodded. "Or this could be a very long three hundred years!

CHAPTER 4

Jorgen Von Strangle looked impatiently at his watch. "I am not having fun yet," he said.

Timmy smiled confidently at his fairy godparents. "Don't worry," he told them. "I got us into this mess, and I'll get us out!"

Timmy walked over to Jorgen. "Say, Jorgen," Timmy began. "How would you like to do something exciting?"

Jorgen smiled. "I love excitement!"

Timmy nodded. "How would you like to do something with a lot of action?" Jorgen smacked his fist into his palm and flexed his giant muscles. "I love action!"

Timmy turned to Cosmo and Wanda. "I wish we were in a Crimson Chin adventure!"

Wanda smiled and waved her wand over her head. "Good thinking, Timmy! One Crimson Chin adventure, coming up!"

There was a shower of magical sparks, and then everything around them changed. Suddenly colors were brighter and bolder. Huge city buildings stood all around. Timmy wore the costume of Cleft, the sidekick to his favorite superhero—the Crimson Chin! They were in a Crimson Chin comic book! Jorgen's Hawaiian shirt was replaced by a superhero costume. He looked down at the symbol on his chest in confusion. "Why is there a giant 'S' on my shirt?"

"Because I'm Cleft, sidekick to the world's greatest hero, the Crimson Chin," Timmy told him. "And you're *my* third sidekick, Stubble! Meet Ace and Clefto, my first two sidekicks," said Timmy, pointing to Cosmo and Wanda.

Jorgen frowned, his eyes narrowing through his mask. "I am a superior officer! I should not be *anyone's* sidekick!"

Timmy rolled his eyes. "Just go with the flow, will you?"

CHAPTER 5

Wanda made a calendar appear and quickly flipped through the pages. "Well, only two hundred and ninety-nine years, eleven months, twenty-nine days, twenty-three hours, and thirty minutes to go," she noted sadly.

Cosmo put his arm around his wife. "I know, our marriage is dragging on," said Cosmo. "I mean, don't worry, Wanda," he reassured her. "I'll come up with a great idea!"

He started to think, absently snapping his fingers as he did. "Cosmo always finds it easier to think when he's snapping his fingers," Wanda told Timmy and Jorgen. After a few moments, however, Cosmo seemed to forget all about thinking and started to dance! "Unfortunately, whenever Cosmo

Jorgen put his hands on his hips. "I am not flowing anywhere until I meet this Crimson Chin person and—OOF!"

Before he could finish, the Crimson Chin fell out of the sky and landed right on top of Jorgen! They fell to the ground in a heap, the Crimson Chin almost crushing Jorgen beneath him.

Timmy quickly helped the Crimson Chin up. "C. C.! What happened?"

The Crimson Chin dusted himself off and looked to the sky. "Glad to see you, Cleft! I'm going to need every friend I can get to tackle this archfiend!"

starts snapping, it sounds like music to him, and he has to dance!"

Cosmo spun, flipped, and jiggled, still snapping his fingers. "Woo-hoo! Everyone should dance twenty-five hours a day," he said. "It's impossible not to have fun when you're dancing!"

Timmy's eyes lit up. "Cosmo, you're a genius!"

Cosmo stopped dancing. "Hey, watch your mouth!" he said with a frown.

"No, 'genius' is good, Cosmo," Wanda told him.

Cosmo sighed with relief. "Whew!"

Timmy huddled with his fairy godparents. "Since everyone has fun dancing, let's teach Jorgen some steps!"

Cosmo lifted his wand. "That's a great idea! I really *am* a genius!"

POOF! Suddenly all four of them were in a big music hall with wooden planks for floors and a band wearing overalls and cowboy hats on the stage. They held instruments like banjos and fiddles. "Howdy, folks," one of the band members said into a microphone. "Welcome to the big square dance!

It's time to get movin'! Choose your partners!"

Cosmo faced Wanda, and Timmy faced Jorgen, who looked back at him, confused. "Just go with the flow," Timmy told him.

Jorgen shook his head again. "I will not go with the flow until—OOF!" Before he could finish, Timmy had grabbed him by the elbow and spun him around so fast that Jorgen got dizzy!

"That's right," sang the man with the microphone. "Swing your partner if you please, now kindly tickle him on his knees!"

Cosmo, Wanda, and Timmy followed all of the band's singsong commands, laughing and having a great time!

"Jump and flip if you don't mind, kick yourself in your own behind!"

Timmy and his fairy godparents danced to the band's music as it got faster and faster. But Timmy noticed Jorgen wasn't laughing, dancing, or smiling. "What's the matter?" he wanted to know.

Without answering, Jorgen walked to the stage. "You are a terrible commander," Jorgen told the

singer. "You should never say 'please' or 'if you don't mind.' You must *order*, firmly!"

He took the microphone from the singer and barked into it, "March!"

Cosmo, Wanda, and Timmy started to march.

"Lift those knees, or it's no joke," Jorgen sang, "you'll be marching till you choke!"

Sweating from the hard work, Timmy turned to look at Cosmo and Wanda. "I don't think dancing was such a good idea either," he told them.

"I think it's time we changed the tune," Cosmo agreed, waving his wand.

POOF! They were back in Timmy's room once more. Jorgen stood over them, shaking his head. "I know it has been a long time since I have taken a vacation," said Jorgen, looking disappointed. "But I remember them being more fun than this," he said sadly.

CHAPTER 6

"Why is it that Jorgen's vacation is making *me* tense?" Cosmo wanted to know.

"I know what you mean," Timmy told him. "I'm so frustrated, I can't think of anything fun for us to try!"

Wanda smiled, getting ready to wave her wand. "That's it! We need to relax! And there's no better place to relax than at the Fairy World spa!"

POOF! Suddenly all four of them were in the bright sunshine, standing by a giant pool, holding glasses of lemonade with little umbrellas stuck in them.

But Jorgen looked bored. "What do we do now?" he asked.

Wanda lay back and put her hands behind her

head. "Now we just take it easy and enjoy the sunshine!"

Jorgen conjured up a white bodysuit that covered him from head to toe. "Too much sun is very bad for you," he told them.

Timmy sighed. "Okay, sunbathing is not an option. What else do people do at a spa?"

Wanda thought a little more, then smiled. "I know! We could take a class here! Maybe one of those fancy classes with stretching exercises! That's supposed to be very relaxing!"

"I'll just watch," Cosmo said, flexing his biceps. "I'm already ripped, shredded, firmed, toned, and totally solid!" His biceps sagged down below his elbows, swinging loosely back and forth. Cosmo blushed. "Then again, a little exercise never hurt anybody!"

POOF! Now they were in a large room with mirrors on the walls, lying on foam mats. At the front of the room sat an odd little man in a tank top and shorts. "Welcome to class," he said. "My exercises will not only relax you, they will stretch you in ways you have never been stretched and make you very strong!"

He moved on the mat, balancing on one finger, and twisted himself into a pretzel shape with one leg up around the back of his neck and his other arm behind his back! He smiled at them. "Please do exactly as I do. This position is called 'Uncomfortable Ferret in a Hailstorm.'"

Timmy tried to get his leg up over his head. He even used both hands. But it was no use. He looked over at Cosmo and Wanda—they had accidentally tied themselves together in a giant knot!

Then Timmy looked over at Jorgen. He was balancing easily on one finger—and doing push-ups! "This is too easy," he growled. "I do not need this stretching class to become stronger! I am already strong!"

"So much for taking a class," Timmy said as he untied his fairy godparents. "We're going to have to get creative in thinking of ways to relax!"

Wanda's eyes lit up. "Creative? Timmy, that's perfect!" She waved her wand again.

POOF!

CHAPTER 7

Timmy looked around and saw that he, Jorgen, and Wanda were all wearing berets and standing before easels. Like his companions, Timmy had a pallet of paint in one hand and a brush in the other.

"We'll try painting," Wanda suggested. "It's creative *and* relaxing!"

Jorgen looked around. "Where is Cosmo? Won't he be painting with us?"

Cosmo stepped before the easels wearing a bathrobe. "I won't be painting—I'll be your model!" And with that he dropped the robe! Timmy clapped his hands over his eyes—he didn't want to see Cosmo without any clothes on!

"Timmy? Is everything all right?" Wanda wanted to know.

Timmy peeked between his fingers. Cosmo wasn't naked; he had magically turned into a bowl of fruit! Timmy blushed and picked up his brush.

When he was finished with his painting, Timmy looked over at Jorgen. Jorgen was simply staring at his canvas, which was still blank. "Aren't you going to paint anything?" Timmy asked.

"I was just about to start," Jorgen said. Then he took his pallet and smashed it into the canvas!

"That's . . . really interesting," Wanda managed to say. "It's very . . . abstract."

Jorgen took off his hat and wiped his paint-covered hands on it. "The problem with painting," he said, "is that it's over before you can really relax!"

"Okay, painting is out." Timmy sighed, turning to Cosmo, who had now turned into a vase of flowers. "What should we try next?"

"How about a nature hike?" Cosmo suggested. "We could look at trees, bushes, birds, squirrels, and race cars!"

Wanda raised her eyebrows. "That sounds great, but . . . race cars? You don't usually see race cars when you're out on a nature hike, Cosmo."

"I know," Cosmo said. "That's why I always bring mine with me!" He raised his wand, and—

POOF! Timmy found himself scrunched into a car seat between Cosmo and Wanda, with Jorgen sitting by the passenger window. The car was moving so fast, Timmy could barely open his eyes!

"Waaaaaa-hooooooo!" Cosmo yelled from behind the steering wheel.

Timmy managed to force his eyes open enough

to see that he was inside a cramped race car! Through the windshield he could see that the car was speeding through a forest, zipping through trees, barely missing them, and barely missing several scared animals that leapt out of the way just in the nick of time!

"Squirrel!" Cosmo cried, pointing out the side of the car as they raced by the terrified animal.

"C-C-Cosmo," Wanda stammered, looking as scared as Timmy felt, "Aren't we going a little fast?"

"You *have* to go fast," Cosmo replied. "That way you can see more nature!" He swerved again and pointed. "Monkey!"

"Stop the car, Cosmo!" Jorgen suddenly yelled.

Cosmo brought the car to a screeching stop and looked over at Jorgen, worried.

"You zigged back there when you should have zagged," Jorgen told him. "And what should you have done when you zagged?"

Cosmo thought about it for a long moment. Then he shrugged. "I should have zurgged?"

"No!" Jorgen said, slamming his fist into the dashboard. "You should have zigged!"

"So much for nature hikes," Wanda said, sighing.

"I don't feel any more relaxed," Cosmo said. "In fact, I feel like I've been tackled by an entire football team!"

That gave Timmy a great idea. "Massages! They're supposed to relax you, right?"

Cosmo and Wanda both nodded eagerly.

POOF!

Timmy found himself lying on his stomach on a long table. He couldn't see what was going on anywhere else in the room, but he could feel someone chopping the sides of their hands into his back! "H-h-h-hey," he stuttered. "W-w-w-w-what's g-g-g-going on?"

"Th-th-th-these are our massages," he heard Wanda say from the table next to him. "Isn't it w-w-w-w-wonderful?"

Timmy, Cosmo, and Wanda all looked up from their tables at Jorgen. Like them, he was flat on his stomach, and a muscular masseur was about to start giving the fairy godparent supervisor his own massage. The masseur cracked his knuckles and flexed his fingers, preparing to work.

Finally he raised his hand to begin chopping the muscles on Jorgen's back, and he brought his hand down. But Jorgen's muscles were too tight! The masseur's hand smacked Jorgen's back then bounced off, sending the masseur stumbling back across the room, his hand throbbing in pain! "Owie," the masseur squeaked.

The masseurs who had been working on Timmy, Cosmo, and Wanda gathered around their injured friend and helped him out of the room. Jorgen sat up, rolling his head on his shoulders and frowning. "If that was a massage, then it was most unsatisfactory," Jorgen told them. "In fact, this entire vacation has been most unsatisfactory! I am beginning to wish I had never taken a vacation . . . and that I did not share it with you!"

Cosmo, Wanda, and Timmy hung their heads. "I feel bad," Timmy said to his fairy godparents. "It was my idea to have Jorgen spend his vacation with us, and we haven't found anything fun for him to do!"

"Even worse," Cosmo pointed out, "now we have to spend the next three hundred years listening to Jorgen complain about it!"

CHAPTER 9

Back in Timmy's room, Timmy, Cosmo, and Wanda tried hard to think of something else that might be fun for Jorgen. Crimson Chin adventures were fun for Timmy, but not for Jorgen. Cosmo liked to dance, but Jorgen didn't. Wanda enjoyed going to the spa, but that definitely wasn't something Jorgen liked. And he didn't like painting or nature hikes, either! Jorgen didn't seem to like anything!

"We could go hang gliding," Cosmo suggested.

"No, Jorgen would find something wrong with his equipment, or his parachute wouldn't fit," Wanda predicted.

"We could play kickball," Cosmo offered.

"No, Jorgen would probably kick a big hole in the ball. And then he would complain that the ball wasn't strong enough," Wanda said, sighing.

Timmy looked at Jorgen, who was magically rearranging the books on Timmy's bookshelf into alphabetical order. Timmy shook his head. Jorgen couldn't help fixing things if he thought something was wrong!

"We have to do something," Timmy said urgently to Cosmo and Wanda. "Tomorrow Francis is going to pick on my friends and me the same way he did today, and we won't ever be able to do anything about it if we're always worrying about Jorgen having a good time!"

"Hmm," Cosmo said, scratching his chin. "Maybe we could ask Francis to wait another three hundred years before bothering you!"

"Francis will never do that," Timmy told him. "He can't count to three hundred."

Having finished rearranging the books, Jorgen turned around. He didn't look happy. "Cosmo and Wanda, I have prepared a review of your performance so far on this vacation," he barked. With a burst of magical sparks, diagrams, charts, and statistics appeared before him. "Cosmo! You are holding your wand thirty percent too low! You must angle your elbow more!"

Cosmo quickly took out a notepad and a pen and took notes. "More . . . angle . . ." he said as he wrote. "Yes, sir!"

"Wanda," Jorgen continued. "You must sweep the wand, like this!" He demonstrated, swooping his arm over his head.

"Sweep, yes, sir!" Wanda replied, trying it. She swept so far that she turned herself upside down and her crown fell off.

Frustrated, tired, and angry, Timmy interrupted Jorgen in mid lesson. "Leave Cosmo and Wanda alone," Timmy shouted. "This whole time we've done nothing but try to help you have a good time!"

"Timmy," Cosmo and Wanda warned in a whisper, not wanting Timmy to make their boss any angrier. Jorgen frowned and his face turned red. He did not like being yelled at.

Timmy didn't pay any attention to the warning. He was fed up and continued to yell at Jorgen. "But all you've done is complain and criticize everything we've done! It's like that's all you know how to do, or all you like to do!"

Jorgen's face turned back to its normal color, and his mighty muscles sagged. He looked at the ground. "That *is* all I like to do," he said. "That is what makes me happiest! I guess you are right . . . I am just not cut out for vacations!"

Timmy paused for a breath and thought about everything he had just said. Then he smiled. He had the best idea of all! "Cosmo, Wanda, I just figured it out! I know exactly what we should do!"

Cosmo and Wanda looked fearfully at Jorgen. He was so sad, it looked like his face might droop off and splatter on the floor. "We should apologize," Wanda said.

"Or we should run, in case he gets angry again," Cosmo said.

"No," Timmy told them, "I need to make a wish . . . and I wish that Jorgen's vacation was already over!"

Cosmo scratched his head. "Why didn't I think of that? *I'm* the genius!"

Cosmo and Wanda looked at each other and smiled. Cosmo raised his wand at a perfect angle. Wanda swept her arm over her head just as Jorgen had showed her.

POOF!

When the sparks cleared, Jorgen was wearing his military clothes again and holding his suitcases. He had a smile on his face. "Now that my vacation is over, I must be getting back to work," he told them. "It's hard to believe it has been three hundred years already. Timmy, you haven't aged a bit."

"All this vacation has kept me young," Timmy said, winking.

Jorgen stepped through the door into Fairy World. He bowed to Cosmo, Wanda, and Timmy. "Good-bye. Thank you for spending my vacation with me. I am actually looking forward to working again," he admitted. "Work is what I enjoy more than anything else. But it took this break for me to realize it. I don't think I'll be taking another one for at least three hundred more years!" With that he stepped through the door, and it closed behind him.

Cosmo, Wanda, and Timmy high-fived each other! Wanda let out a deep breath. "Whew! I'm glad that's over!"

Cosmo clapped Timmy on the back. "Great thinking, Timmy! After all that work, now *we* need a vacation!"

Timmy shook his head, pointing to his watch. "Not yet," he said. "We have to get back to my school tomorrow! Francis is probably at home practicing his towel snaps!"

"Okay, but we really shouldn't steal his towel," Wanda told him. "That's still against Da Rules."

Timmy nodded gloomily. "I guess you're right," he admitted. Then he smiled. "Hey, how about if we let Francis keep his towel . . . but turn his bathing suit into *spaghetti sauce?*"

Cosmo and Wanda smiled, raising their wands. "*That* we can do!" Wanda said.

POOF!

ABOUT THE AUTHOR

Adam Beechen hasn't taken a vacation in a long, long time. He's too busy writing books, comics, and television cartoons! Adam lives in Los Angeles, California.

ABOUT THE ILLUSTRATOR

Barry Goldberg has illustrated over seventy books for children, including books based on *The Fairly OddParents* and *SpongeBob SquarePants*. He lives in Long Island, NY.

READ MORE ADVENTURES STARRING *TIMMY TURNER!*

TIMMY TURNER, ACTION HERO

With a *poof!* the tree house was instantly transformed. Splintery wooden walls became computers. Posters turned into electronic view screens. Wooden barrels and crates became high-tech command chairs with real cup holders!

The sliding doors opened with a swish. Timmy, A.J., and Chester raced into the control center and took their positions. A.J. manned the view screens. Chester armed the weapons system.

Still clutching his Crimson Chin action figure, Timmy sat in the command chair in the center of the room. As he hopped into the seat, Timmy pressed a red button on the armrest. Out popped Wanda and

Cosmo, still inside their fishbowl and still looking like goldfish. No one, not even Timmy's best friends, could know about his fairy godparents.

A.J. twirled a dial. "Enemy on-screen, Captain," he announced. An image of Tootie appeared on a large-screen television, even bigger than life. She still gripped the picture of Timmy. But now the photo was soggy from all the wet, slobbery kisses she had showered on it.

Timmy saw the image on the screen and shuddered. Then he held his Crimson Chin action figure high above his head.

"Prepare to fire phasers!" ordered Timmy.

Chester pressed a button. A giant slingshot popped out of the tree house window. The band was stretched tight, ready to fire.

"Phasers locked, Captain," said Chester grimly.

Inside the fishbowl, Cosmo's eyes bugged out. "I love when the phasers get locked," he cried.

On the television screen, Tootie was yelling.

"Tiiiiimmy! Can I come up and play?"

"Fire!" Timmy commanded.

Chester pressed the launch button. With a *boing,* the slingshot let loose. A big red water balloon flew at Tootie. At the last second the balloon stopped in midair. It spun around over Tootie's head, then burst. Instantly Tootie was soaked with cold water.

"Waaa!" Tootie howled. "I'm so wet, you can't even see how much I'm crying!"

Up in the tree house, the boys cheered.

Tootie, still shrieking, looked up at them. "Can I at least come up and dry off?" she cried.

But Timmy showed Tootie no mercy. After Chester automatically reloaded the slingshot, Timmy yelled out another command.

"Fire!"

This time Tootie saw the balloon coming. When it paused in flight to spin over her head, she stepped out from under it.

Unfortunately for Tootie, Cosmo and Wanda had made these water balloons magical. The balloon moved over Tootie's head, then exploded with a *splat.* "Waaa! Waaa!" sobbed Tootie, dripping wet.

"Yeah!" cheered Timmy, Chester, and A.J. as

they slapped palms in a high five.

But their celebration was interrupted by an urgent beeping. The sound was coming from the slingshot control panel.

"Darn it!" said Chester. "We're all out of balloons!"

A.J. grinned. "Let's go get some more, and we can strap the Crimson Chin down to one!"

Timmy looked at his action figure. "Yeah!" he said with a big smile. "We can hit Tootie with a balloon *and* a plastic doll!"

"Waaaaa!" Tootie howled from outside.

A.J. and Chester raced for the exit.

Timmy's friends were gone, and now he was alone with his action figure.

"Well, I guess this is good-bye," Timmy said to the Crimson Chin. Then he pressed the button on the Chin's plastic chest.

"You're my best pal!" the action figure said.

Timmy's smile vanished. Suddenly he felt bad about trashing his once-favorite toy.

Just then Cosmo and Wanda turned back

into fairies and floated out of their fishbowl. "If you used to like it so much, why are you going to destroy it?" Cosmo asked.

Timmy shrugged. "Because I don't need this doll anymore. I have you guys!" Then Timmy gave the Crimson Chin a second look. "Still, he *was* pretty cool," Timmy admitted.

Wanda and Cosmo smiled at each other. They knew exactly what Timmy was going to say!

"You know," Timmy said, "I wish I could play with him one more time."

Wanda fired a magical bolt at Timmy, and Cosmo directed his magical energy at the Crimson Chin action figure.

Poof! Poof!

"Hey!" squeaked Timmy in a tiny voice. "I'm toy-size!"

Then the Crimson Chin doll landed right next to Timmy, who was still seated on the now-giant command chair.

"There's evil afoot! I mean, a-chin!" bellowed the Crimson Chin in a bold, manly voice.

"Wow!" said Timmy, his eyes wide. "You made him come alive!"

"Sure," Cosmo replied. "Sitting next to a lifeless doll would have been boring."